The Cat's Meow

Designed by:
Sally Reed, The Quick Brown Fox

Published by:
PublishingWorks
60 Winter Street
Exeter, NH 03833
603-778-9883

Marketing and Sales by Revolution Booksellers.

LCN: 2006902972

ISBN: 1-933002-14-X

Printed in Canada

The Cat's Meow

Teri Mgrdichian
Illustrated by Gertie McGlinchey

PUBLISHINGWORKS
EXETER, NH
2006

Dedication

To Mark, you are my everything.

To Mom and Dad, you have made me what I am.

*To Jeremy, Zach, Darren, Cassie and Hannah,
you have been my best and most honest critics. Thank you!!!*

Markey and Brian......Just Thank You for being. I love You.

–TM–

This work is dedicated to my husband, Jim, my constant supporter...

To my daughter, Teri, the author and inspiration.

*And to the numerous smiley faces who are yet to enjoy this story
and its attending pictures.*

–GM–

The
CAT'S
MEOW

A long time ago, in a magical land called Belief, there lived a wizard named Mao Li Tse Khu.

He shared his tiny home with his friend, Sir Mouse, who had sailed across the ocean on a leaf.

One day, as Mao and Sir Mouse sat on a sandy beach they met a cat named Winsome. The three began to talk as they watched the birds flying over the ocean.

"I could do that," boasted the cat, pointing up to the birds.

Sir Mouse laughed out loud. "Do you mean you could fly?" He laughed harder.

"You cannot," said Mao quietly.

"I'll bet you I could," said Winsome, not understanding what could be so hard about flying.

Mao looked down at Winsome, and frowned.

"On my name, I will bet you cannot," said Mao, as Sir Mouse giggled behind him.

Winsome walked away from the beach wondering

why Mao insisted he could not fly.

"How hard could it be?" he asked himself as he lay down beside a small pond.

All of that night he dreamed of flying.

Suddenly, something hit Winsome in the head. Hard.

"Wake up!" a voice cried. "What are you doing sleeping by my pond?"

The cat opened his eyes and saw a loon floating before him, looking sour.

"I'm sorry, Mr. Loon," he apologized. "I didn't know that this was your pond."

"Humph," Mr. Loon snorted and turned to paddle away.

"Wait! Mr. Loon, I have a question!" Winsome

called. Mr. Loon turned back.

"Mr. Loon, could you teach me to fly?" the cat asked.

Mr. Loon laughed.

"Silly boy, you can't fly without wings," he said, waving one wing at him.

Then Mr. Loon flew away, leaving Winsome alone on the shore.

Winsome spent the rest of the day watching Mr. Loon and his friends flying around the pond. Slowly, he began to see what Mr. Loon was talking about. He looked at his reflection in the water and saw that he did not have any wings.

"This could be a big problem," he thought.

Late in the afternoon, Mr. Loon and his friends flew away to another loon's pond to visit. Winsome slowly walked back toward Mao's house. He stood in the doorway and listened as Mao described a beautiful place called Rome to Sir Mouse.

Winsome sighed. It sounded like a perfect place to fly over.

He coughed softly and both Mao and Sir Mouse turned to look at him.

"We need to talk," said Winsome as he walked

back out onto the porch.

Sir Mouse and Mao followed him outside. Sir Mouse sat down and Mao lit a small torch that made magical shapes in its smoke.

"I cannot fly," Winsome said quietly.

Sir Mouse smiled, but Mao simply nodded.

"Without those wing things that Mr. Loon told me about, I just cannot fly. And besides, who ever heard of a flying cat? It's silly!" he cried.

Sir Mouse had started to giggle, but Mao just nodded.

"Well, I lost the bet fair and square," Winsome sighed. "I'm ready to pay up."

Sir Mouse laughed loudly, but then quickly backed up when he saw the look on the wizard's face.

"Sir Mouse," Mao hissed. "You have been behaving very badly these last days and I think you need to be taught a lesson. Let's see how the other mice will feel when they find out that because of your teasing of the cat all mice can now only make one sound."

Without warning Mao spun around, raised his arms and cast his spell on Winsome and Sir Mouse.

"Zhrak!" he roared. Sir Mouse squeaked in fear and ran into the house.

Mao reached down and stroked Winsome's head. "Things will be a little different now. Sir Mouse chose his sound when I cast my spell so now he and all other mice will be able to only squeak. And all you can say is my name."

Mao scratched Winsome behind the ear.

Sir Mouse ran wildly across the porch and into the yard, squeaking all the way.

"You see," Mao said. "If Sir Mouse had been nicer to you... well, he wasn't, so now he can just squeak. As I said before, you did try, but a bet's a bet, and you lost."

"Think back, Winsome. I told you that I would bet you on my name. Never make bets with a wizard! For although you could win," Mao smiled, "You, Winsome, you lose some, too."

And all the
cat could say
was "Mao."

TERI MGRDICHIAN started writing short stories in the sixth grade when her English teacher told her she was good. She stopped writing in college when her English Composition professor told her she had no talent. Four years later, on a whim, she wrote a children's poem called "The Cat's Meow," which eventually became this book. Teri resides in Raymond, NH, with her husband Mark, stepsons Mark and Brian, and their loyal canine companion, Shakespeare.

GERTIE MCGLINCHEY has "played" with drawing and painting for sixty years. She is the mother of Teri Mgrdichian, the author. She lives in New Hampshire with her husband of forty-two years, Jim. Her favorite work is pet portraits, which she does by commission. Currently, she and Jim are editors for the Seacoast Artists Association newsletter in Exeter, New Hampshire.